D1103466

THIS BOOK BELONGS TO:

Miaow!

Mick Inkpen

A division of Hodder Headline Limited

Kipper and Tiger were looking for conkers when they heard a noise.

'Miaow!'

There was a kitten in the conker tree.

'Are you stuck?' said Kipper.

Kipper climbed on to Tiger's shoulders to reach the kitten.

He grabbed the nearest branch. . .

. . .which snapped!

'Conkers!' said Tiger.

'Wait there!' said Kipper.
'I'm going to get my
blanket, to catch the kitten.'
So Tiger watched the
kitten and counted
his conkers.

On the way back,
Kipper met Pig and
his little cousin, Arnold.
'There's a kitten in the
conker tree!' he said.
'Come and help!'

'Jump into my blanket!'
said Kipper.
'Miaow!' said the kitten.
It wouldn't jump.

Arnold climbed up inside the tree.

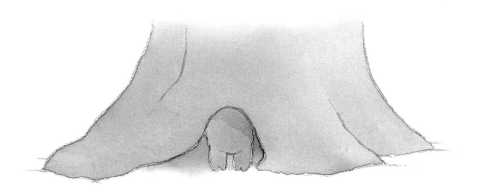

He walked along the branch.

He sat down and
stroked the kitten.

He showed it how to
jump into the blanket.

The kitten got up.
'He's going to jump!'
shouted Kipper.

But the kitten did not
jump. It trotted along the
branch. . .

. . .and climbed down
inside the tree.

Then it flicked
its tail and
went home.
'It wasn't stuck
at all!' said Kipper.

First published 2000
by Hodder Children's Books,
a division of Hodder Headline Limited,
338 Euston Road, London NW1 3BH

Copyright © Mick Inkpen 2000

10 9 8 7 6 5 4 3 2 1

ISBN 0 340 75419 2